MARRIED OFF BY THE DUKE

CARRIE LOMAX

Copyright © 2023 by Carrie Lomax

All rights reserved.

No part of this book may be reproduced in any form or by any electronic or mechanical means, including information storage and retrieval systems, without written permission from the author, except for the use of brief quotations in a book review.

This book may not be used to train any Large Language Model database or otherwise used in any artificial intelligence program without the express written permission of the author. No platform has the right to sublicense others to reproduce and/or otherwise use this work in any manner for purposes of training artificial intelligence technologies to generate text without the author's specific and express permission.

This is a work of fiction. All characters, events, and most locations are invented by the author; any resemblance to actual people, places and events are typically coincidental, except actual place names such as cities and countries.

Cover art by Forever After Romance.

eBook ASIN: B0CRQ1ZBXC

eBook ISBN: 9798224829149

Print ISBN: 9798874469948

LONDON, SPRING OF 1882

CHAPTER 1

You shall endeavor to find a husband at the earliest opportunity, read the letter from her guardian.

"I will do no such thing," Emma muttered, and tossed the crumpled ball into the fire. A pity that her thoughts could not reduce its author to ash along with it. Lord Maximus Aloysius Tremaine, the sixth Duke of Ardennes, deserved to burn for eternity.

Or longer.

Unfortunately, Emma had no power to send her cursed guardian anywhere. He, however, had the authority to order her anywhere he wished, and the duke was not afraid to wield it.

Where he wanted her right now was in London for her first Season. He couldn't have been more insulting about it if he'd tried.

I have neglected your situation long enough. Between your piddling dowry and your advanced age, you will be lucky to attract any suitor at all. Leaving it for another year won't do.

As if she were some sort of fancy lady instead of the illegitimate daughter of an earl's second son.

Emma was accustomed to being unwanted. At least the previous Duke of Ardennes had been a kindly man. His son, the current duke, was a different story. Max had treated her with arrogance and disdain from the moment they first met. Until now, he'd been content to let her molder away in the countryside, out of sight and out of mind.

Summoning her away from school in the middle of the spring term would impact her students. As if her teaching didn't matter.

To the Duke of Ardennes, it didn't. Nothing mattered except his whims. Inexplicably, he'd decided now was the time to divest himself of responsibility for her welfare. No doubt he would hand-select London's most loathsome toad for her husband. On purpose.

Why?

She wasn't a troublesome ward. They rarely interacted.

Clearly, the duke despised her more than she'd ever imagined.

"Likewise," Emma muttered, watching the paper crumble into ash. "I certainly won't be shackling myself to the first man who asks, simply to appease His Grace-lessness."

While she didn't want a Season, she did want to be free from her pompous, arrogant guardian forever, ideally before she was legally emancipated at the age of twenty-five. On this point, they were in profound agreement.

Unless…

What if she could frustrate him into granting her control over her inheritance early?

A diabolical plan unfolded in her mind. Max's desperation to be rid of her presented Emma with an opportunity.

She felt certain she was up to the challenge of annoying Max into granting her freedom on a much quicker timeline than the four years she would otherwise have to wait. Matrimony was out of the question. Emma was done with being a perpetual burden to others. She had no intention of locking herself into a loveless marriage for the duke's convenience.

"Miss Willis, your carriage is here," the headmaster informed her.

"I am ready."

Ready to wage war.

CHAPTER 2

Max eyed Miss Willis' plain gown and unflattering bonnet with skepticism. He'd sent her funds for adequate clothing before the school year started, but she hadn't spent a farthing of it, apparently.

Marrying off Willful Miss Willis might be harder than he'd anticipated, and he hadn't expected marrying off his vexing ward to be easy. He'd already put it off until the Season was well underway.

"An appointment with a dressmaker is the first order of business."

"Is that how you welcome visitors these days?" she asked acerbically.

"Men like pretty women, not dowdy vipers." Emma's features were delicate; whenever she wasn't scowling, she wasn't unappealing. Still, her appearance could be improved with a decent dress and a bit of deft hairstyling…

"Thank you for that scathing assessment. I don't have much need for evening gowns at Mrs. Quarrie's School for the Improvement of Young Ladies. Did you need me for anything other than as a target for your insults, Your Graceless…erm, Your Grace? Or may I be excused? I am quite fatigued."

Max sighed. Miss Willis' head barely came to his shoulder. Kissing her would involve craning one's neck at an uncomfortable angle—

Inwardly, he groaned. *Not this, again.*

Max couldn't stop his physical reaction to his ward. He'd never been able to tamp it down, a fact that had befuddled him for the entirety of their acquaintance.

Her lilting voice tumbled around in his mind for several seconds before her words clicked into place.

"Did you just call me Your Graceless?"

Pink stained Emma's creamy cheeks. There was a small mark near the left side of her mouth. He couldn't stop staring at it. Max often found himself distracted by the lush shape and color of her lips.

When Miss Willis was around, he couldn't bloody *think*.

"What if I did?" she asked bluntly.

Max rubbed his temples.

"It's actually, 'Your Gracelessness,'" she informed him.

"Pot, meet kettle." Max had the absurd impulse to laugh.

"I am no duchess. I am therefore not expected to display any grace, Your Gracelessness."

"Grace is inherent to the female sex. The exception proves the rule, I suppose." Seeing the protest form on her rosebud lips, he cut her off by saying, "I reckon you're wondering why I called you home."

"Ardennes House isn't my home."

Max's headache abruptly worsened. "Away from the school, then."

"You were rather blunt in stating your reasons. Shall I repeat them?"

"Not necessary, I remember them perfectly—"

"'Miss Willis, the occasion of your recent birthday reminds me how your marital prospects decline with each passing day. Already, you are sufficiently aged that finding a suitor will be no easy feat, particularly given your deficient personal charms—'"

"Did you memorize my entire letter?" he demanded, aghast. He felt certain that wasn't what he'd actually written. The *deficient personal charms* bit did sound disturbingly familiar, though.

Max hadn't considered what it might feel like to receive such a letter. He was a duke, and unaccustomed to considering anyone else's feelings about anything at all.

"Every. Word." Miss Willis took two steps forward. Her extended index finger prodded him in the sternum. Max flinched. "Before I burned it."

She crossed her arms over her chest.

"At least you've done me the courtesy of destroying the evidence of my poor manners." He stood stiffly, flexing his hands so as not to make fists.

Emma smirked.

He wanted to…to…*do something* to make it stop. His immediate impulse was to kiss her, but that would earn him a slap, so he imagined throttling her instead.

"I burn all your letters, Your Grace."

He sighed. "Funnily enough, I save all of yours."

She frowned. A matching expression stole over his face. Why would he admit such a thing? To her, of all people?

"This guardianship business must end."

"I concur. Grant me my inheritance and let me go my own way," Emma said brightly.

Max snorted. "No. However, since neither of us finds joy in each other's company, let us find a way to quit this arrangement."

"The fastest way to do that would be to give me what's mine and let me go."

"You're a woman."

"You noticed!"

Max's jaw tightened. Yes, he had noticed she was a woman from their very first encounter. Technically, Emma was no beauty. No individual aspect stood out as an exceptional trait. Taken together, though, the whole of her composition tempted him more than any other woman he'd ever met.

Her small frame was well-proportioned, though her torso was regrettably concealed by a high neckline. Max did enjoy a nice bosom, and he'd been curious about hers for six long, frustrating years.

Her hair might be an unremarkable shade of brown, but it was sleek and thick, like a mink's fur. His hand lifted involuntarily as if to stroke it. Horrified, Max clasped his hands behind his back to prevent them from wandering.

"I have no doubt you, like any woman, would fritter away your inheritance within weeks, thus forcing me to rescue you from your own folly. No ward of mine ends up in the workhouse, no matter how irresponsible she is. I won't have your behavior reflecting poorly upon me."

An outraged gasp. For once, Miss Willis' quick tongue appeared to be momentarily tied. Max pressed the advantage.

"You shall therefore endeavor to find a husband at the earliest available opportunity. Understood?"

"Or what?"

"What do you mean, what?" Max thought he'd been perfectly clear on this point.

"What if I don't wish to marry? What will you do to me if I defy you?"

He laughed. Emma's cheeks flushed red.

"You have no hold over me besides money," she said. "Give me what's mine and let me go. I'll never darken your doorstep again."

His laughter ebbed. A strange feeling twisted in his stomach. He should do it. There was no one stopping him from handing her a small pile of banknotes and being rid of her for good.

But if he did, he'd never see her pale blue eyes light up with mischief again.

A lump lodged painfully behind his sternum.

"Money, Miss Willis, is the only thing standing between you and destitution. I think you'll find that living without it is highly uncomfortable."

"You wouldn't know."

"No. Nor do I intend to find out. I have no appetite for bed lice, thin gruel and holes in the soles of my boots, which is what you would find in a workhouse. I enjoy being comfortable. Believe it or not, I want the same comforts for you. My father promised to provide for you and protect you until your twenty-fifth birthday or marriage, whichever came first. I do not wish to endure four more years of guardianship any more than you do."

She stiffened as if he'd struck her.

"Since I am so odious to Your Gracelessness, I shall remove myself from your exalted presence forthwith."

Emma stormed away in a swirl of skirts. Max blew out a breath. That had gone even worse than expected, and his expectations had not been high.

One thing was certain: he had no control where Miss Willis was concerned. None. The sooner she was out of his life, the better.

For both of them.

CHAPTER 3

Carriage rides were the worst part of Emma's thus-far unspectacular season, for the sole reason that they forced her into proximity with her loathsome guardian. Tonight, he was taking her to a soirée to meet a widowed judge.

"Try smiling," Max commanded.

Emma bared her teeth in a wolfish snarl.

"Not like that."

She let her face relax, then nearly toppled off the seat when her guardian mumbled, "You're pretty when you smile," while staring determinedly out the window of the coach. He shifted uncomfortably. "Prettier, I mean."

"Was that a compliment?"

"An unintentional one, I assure you."

She didn't know what to do with a compliment falling from his lips. Since when had he thought her even marginally attractive?

Since never. It was another joke. That's all.

Several tense minutes passed in silence. Emma kept glancing at Max, trying to make sense of what he'd said.

Why did nature bless the most devilish men with the most angelic faces? She could hardly tear her gaze away from the sculpted angularity of his features, even though it pinched her heart to look at him.

A small, stupid part of her preened to think that a man like Max thought her pretty. Emma knew better. She'd seen the kind of women who fawned over him. Dazzling beauties dripping in gemstone jewelry. A duke was a rare catch indeed.

Looking closer at her guardian now, Emma frowned. His Gracelessness appeared pained and faintly green.

"Are you alright?"

"I dislike facing backward in a carriage." He pressed a fist to his lips. "It makes me ill."

"Oh." Emma gasped, startled that her nemesis would admit such frailty. "Switch seats with me. I don't mind facing the rear."

"No." The duke sat straighter. "It isn't done."

"Why not?" Emma demanded.

"Because I'm a gentleman. I ride this way. You're a lady. You ride that way."

"For pity's sake." *Lord, save me from stubborn men.* "Is this why you've refused to accompany me anywhere? Because you get motion sickness riding backward in a carriage?"

Apart from brief excursions, he'd mostly left Emma to her own devices. Sparring with him at mealtimes, oddly enough, had become the highlight of her day.

"I do not get motion sickness. I get…queasy. That's all."

"Fine. Molder over there like a turnip, then. Whatever you wish to call it, if you must be sick, please at least do so out the window."

Beads of sweat broke out on his brow. Oh, dear. He really was feeling ill. Emma experienced a bewildering pang of sympathy for him.

"I insist upon trading places, Your Grace. I promise no one will ever know how your manhood has been compromised by exchanging seats with a woman for a single carriage ride."

Still, he didn't move, the obstinate arse.

"Oh, do get up." Emma seized his hand and tugged. It was like yanking on a piece of meat. The one time she'd been asked to assist in the kitchen at the school, she'd been sent to fetch a ham from storage. She couldn't figure out how to heft the thing, forcing her to return in shame and admit defeat. Imagine the indignity of losing to a dead pig.

She felt the same things now. When the duke didn't move, Emma dropped his hand.

"Fine. Be that way. I'm going to make space for you to sit on this side, whether you like it or not." Emma crouched to keep her balance on the swaying floor and wedged herself onto the seat beside him. Max jerked away.

Of all the awkward silences that had ever existed, this had to be the longest. Heat from his body seeped into her side. He really was an enormous man. Easily a foot taller than she, and muscular beneath the layers of fine silk, cotton, and wool that indicated a man in possession of immense wealth.

Emma had never thought about a man's shape before it was pressed against her.

"You are…" The duke's voice sounded strained. Probably from nausea.

"Yes?"

"Too close."

He lurched into the opposite seat. Emma couldn't help but feel slighted. Was being close to her truly so off-putting?

This was the outcome you intended.

"I'll open the window." She fumbled with the latch. "I'm

quite fond of this new dress; I wouldn't like to see it ruined if you cast up your accounts."

"I won't do that," he insisted gruffly. The air wafting in carried odors of manure, soot, and dead animals. Still, it helped. The gray-green pallor gradually receded from the duke's skin.

"I'm glad you like the dress," he said after a long silence.

"I don't, particularly." Emma did, but she wasn't about to admit it.

Wear this, do that, act like a lady at all times. Be quiet and forgettable, but memorable enough to attract a decent suitor.

What an impossible balancing act was expected of women.

If I had my own money—my rightful money—I wouldn't have to pretend to be something I'm not.

But she didn't, and so she did.

"You literally said you didn't want me to ruin it because you liked it."

"Just because I don't want you to soil my new dress doesn't mean I enjoy wearing said garment."

He stared out the window for several moments. Emma had the sinking sense that she'd been the bigger arsehole during this particular skirmish.

"We're here," he declared stiffly after a long silence.

"I have eyes, Your Grace."

Her guardian sighed. Emma couldn't blame him. She was, after all, being intentionally difficult. That was her plan. Why, then, did she feel bad that it was working?

The more he hated her, the sooner he would release her. She just had to grit her teeth and continue being as obnoxious to him as possible.

But tonight, he wasn't making it easy. He wasn't being his usual controlling self. He was almost being…nice.

It was very upsetting.

When the carriage halted, Max snapped, "See that you don't embarrass me this evening, Miss Willis. We are here to introduce you to a man I believe would be an appropriate match for a lady of your station. He is of good character."

"Judge Adkins."

"Yes. You are to smile, laugh, and most importantly, do not insult him. If you can manage to go fifteen minutes without saying anything inappropriate. I confess I have my doubts." Max glanced out the window. "Once that task is accomplished, we shall depart before you can ruin your chances by sharpening your rapier wit on the poor man, or any other potential suitors. Understood?"

"You're optimistic to think there will be one suitor, much less a second."

She stepped down from the carriage without taking his proffered hand.

CHAPTER 4

There was no reason whatsoever to feel put out—however mildly—that Emma had captivated The Honorable Mr. Adkins, a high court judge. Yes, he had children who were older than Miss Willis, but that was nothing out of the ordinary. The man was well settled and could afford to overlook her illegitimate birth and pathetic dowry.

Miss Willis tipped her face up and laughed. Jealousy spiked within him.

Max tried to remember a time when he'd ever heard Emma laugh before. He couldn't. Not once in all the years of their acquaintance. She wasn't humorless. She just never smiled when he was around.

Tonight, her smile lit up the entire room. *Pretty* didn't begin to describe it. He hadn't meant for that compliment to slip out, but it was true. When she wasn't sulking like a surly adolescent, Emma was captivating.

Her maid's hairstyling helped. As did the satin gown trimmed with green and pink silk roses.

This was a version of Miss Willis he didn't know. At all.

Come to think of it, he hadn't made any real effort to get to know her. She was, understandably, wary of him. But if she genuinely hated him, she wouldn't have made him switch places with her in the carriage. Would she?

A strange feeling he couldn't name roiled within him. Whether it was hope or lingering indigestion, Max couldn't be certain.

"Where have you been hiding your ward all these years?" A man's voice startled Max out of his reverie. "I thought you said she was a plain little mouse."

"She is. Look at her, Pindell."

"I am. You've undersold her beauty by a wide margin. You might not find her charming, but I'd quite like an introduction, if you'd be so obliging."

Competition is good, Max reminded himself. Two suitors meant a better chance of finding one who would take Emma off his hands. Max had already inquired about obtaining a special license on behalf of his ward. Theoretically, he could be free of Miss Willis by next week.

Pindell was a far better match than a girl like Emma could expect to make. Max ought to be delighted to introduce them.

He wasn't.

A ball of misgiving lodged behind his sternum as he reluctantly led his friend over to where Emma and Adkins were conversing, heads bowed as if they were old friends, despite having met all of ten minutes ago.

"A sensible man in your position ought to seek an heiress, not an illegitimate nobody," Max grumbled.

Emma's smile faltered.

Pindell cut him a glance. "I am in the fortunate position of being able to choose a wife for non-mercenary considerations. Besides, it's rather presumptuous of you to assume I intend to propose before even having met her."

"Marriages have been based upon less acquaintance."

The way Emma's expression darkened at his approach, then brightened the instant he presented Pindell, twisted knifelike in Max's gut.

※

Emma

"Did he actually say that?" Adkins asked in a low tone of astonishment.

"Indeed," Emma said tightly. "His Grace does not think highly of me."

"I have never known Ardennes to be deliberately cruel. A little too convinced of his own righteousness at times, like most men of his class, but to speak so bluntly of your parentage…"

"He speaks the truth," Emma shrugged. It hurt, but she couldn't deny that she was *an illegitimate nobody*.

"Lord Pindell," Adkins said affably, greeting the newcomer. Pindell's ginger curls and eager, open face were a sharp contrast to Max's glower and looming posture. Emma ignored the duke and gave the newcomer a welcoming smile. A viscount, she was informed.

"Miss Willis. I understand you were a teacher until recently?"

"Yes, at Mrs. Quarrie's School for the Improvement Young Ladies. Working with the girls was such a pleasure," she fibbed. There had been moments of joy while teaching, just not many of them. Emma deliberately shifted to a more neutral subject. "Mr. Adkins was telling me about his new grandson."

"I'm surprised you indulged him," Max interjected. "I didn't think you liked children."

A beat of stunned silence passed.

"Of course I like children. I'm not a monster, Your Grace."

"Only a hoyden."

Prickly anger crawled up her spine. She was going to lose her temper if her guardian didn't shut up. Right now.

Max was deliberately sabotaging her already dubious marital prospects. What was *wrong* with him?

"With all due respect, Ardennes, I haven't witnessed any hoydenish behavior from Miss Willis this evening," Adkins said, tilting his head. "You, on the other hand…"

The effect on Max was almost comical. At first, his scowl deepened. Then he shook himself, like a great bear emerging from a winter hibernation, and the scowl disappeared.

"I suppose that means you wish to marry the girl."

"I daresay I have never met a man so obsessed with the matrimonial state as you are." Pindell grinned and slapped Maximus on the back. "It's almost as if you can't wait to get yourself leg-shackled."

Adkins grimaced.

Emma didn't know where to look, or how to make sense of her guardian's appalling behavior. Technically, she had done everything he asked of her this evening. Smiling hadn't been too difficult, either, once she was out of Max's earshot. She'd even been enjoying herself. Adkins took no offense when she confessed that she wasn't seeking a husband. He then confided that neither was he looking to begin a new family, having just married off his youngest daughter. While Emma seemed like a lovely young woman, the judge had a new grandchild to enjoy, and did not wish to become a father again himself.

His honesty won her favor instantly. From there, they'd chatted amiably until Max and Pindell interrupted them.

Naturally, Max couldn't stand seeing her happy.

He stiffened at Pindell's insinuation of marriage as if it were a great insult. "We're leaving. Miss Willis is tired."

"I have expressed no such complaint," Emma protested.

"You've only just arrived." Adkins had confusion written on his craggy features.

"I've hardly had a chance to speak with her." Pindell flashed her a smile.

"If you wish to speak with her, come to my townhome at half-past two tomorrow precisely. Let's go, Emma." He took her arm, trying to haul her out of the chair, and half succeeded before she shook him off. Max glared at her, then at Pindell. "Only visit *if* your intentions are sincere."

Emma's skin prickled with fury.

Adkins' bushy brows rose. "Intentions? We've only just met Miss Willis—"

"You've seen enough to make up your mind about her," Max snapped. "Any further acquaintance will undoubtedly spoil the illusion."

He seized her hand and hauled her to her feet. This time, Emma didn't dare resist.

"You're embarrassing me," she hissed as he dragged her toward the exit.

"*You* are the one embarrassing *me*."

"How?"

"By…by encouraging those rakehells."

"Adkins isn't a rakehell; he's nearly sixty years old! And it was your idea to introduce us in the first place!"

If she thought he'd glowered before, Emma was disabused of that notion now. *This* was a glower of terrifying proportions. Max said nothing, not even a cursory goodbye to their hostess.

"Aren't you going to take leave properly?" she demanded.

"No," he bit out.

"I suppose one of the many perks of being a duke was that one can storm out and not risk being ostracized for your rudeness, but I do wish you'd consider how your behavior reflects upon me."

Acid burned her innards. How could he do this to her? The entire point of this Season she'd never asked for was to look for a husband, and now that one man had expressed the tiniest crumb of interest, His Gracelessness dragged her forcibly away.

Emma had never been so confused in her life.

Outside, while they were waiting on the steps for his carriage to arrive, Max finally released her. Emma lurched back several steps, tripping over the hem of her skirt. He caught her before she could fall.

"What. Are. You. Doing?" Emma hissed. "Are you insane?"

"You're not going to marry Adkins," the duke ground out. "You're not marrying anyone, except me."

Then he tugged her close and kissed her breathless.

CHAPTER 5

Emma's inner turmoil calmed instantly. Rooted to the spot, she could only tip her face up to meet his warm lips. Her tiny gasp offered him an opening, and he pressed the advantage, sweeping his tongue between her teeth in a shockingly intimate caress. Were it not for his arm around the small of her back, her knees would have given out.

How could a man who made her feel bad every time he opened his mouth, make her feel this good with those same lips?

Emma twined her arms around his neck. She'd never realized how much she needed this. Touch. Intimacy.

Never realized how much her prickliness toward him had been driven by her hurt at feeling unwanted.

"Sweet Emma," he murmured against her temple. "You have tormented and tempted me from the first moment we met. There's no help for it. I must have you for my duchess."

Emma's heartbeats thundered inside her skull. He *wanted her.*

Reality intruded, like hitting the ground after jumping off a roof and thinking for a few exhilarating seconds that she could fly.

This was *Max*. Her nemesis. Handsome, rich, never wanted anything to do with her. *That* Max.

She wasn't about to tie herself to his capricious carelessness forever. Not for all the money in the world.

Gathering her wits, she pressed both hands against his chest and pushed.

"It's always the same with you, Maximus Aloysius Tremaine. You say 'I want' and expect the world to drop everything and give it to you."

"I am a duke, after all."

Emma fought not to laugh. He wore his title so casually, sometimes. She hated to admit she liked anything about Max, but she did enjoy that singular aspect of him.

"That does not give you leave to order me around. You interrupted my perfectly content life at the school and brought me to London, with the stated purpose of washing your hands of me. Now, when your plan to marry me off was poised to work, you change course? Has it ever occurred to you to ask what *I* want?"

They both knew he'd never contemplated what she wanted for a single second.

"Perfectly content?" he scoffed. "You were miserable at that damned school."

Her mouth fell open. "I was not!"

"You absolutely were," he insisted. "Waiting for me to rescue you."

Emma gaped. "You do not honestly believe that."

The carriage arrived then, preventing any further discussion. When she glanced up, Emma was dismayed to find the party guests leaning out the window above, pointing at them and gossiping.

There would be no salvaging her reputation after this. Conniving man.

Emma had no intention of tying herself permanently to Max, dukedom or no. He might think he wanted her hand in marriage, but she knew better.

"You, sir, are the last man I would ever consider marrying."

§♠

Max

EMMA'S DECLARATION CRUSHED HIM.

He'd earned her refusal. He had no rational explanation for his actions this evening. Only a swirl of emotions he could barely make sense of. Taken together, the facts added up to one inescapable conclusion: he was in love with his ward, and had been for some time.

Everything clicked into place.

The moment he'd laid eyes on her during that first Christmas visit, he'd been ready to compose bad poetry about Emma's crystalline blue eyes. Their ages at the time —Emma had been a mere fifteen, he not yet turned twenty-two—precluded any genuine expression of interest, and so he treated her as he might a younger cousin. Or tried to. She'd bristled at his teasing, he'd taken umbrage, and things had spiraled downward from there.

Tonight, he'd seen that his ward wasn't a dowdy shrew, but a beautiful young woman who would have no difficulty finding a husband.

He'd almost squandered his chance with her.

Max handed her into the carriage. When Emma pointedly took the rear-facing seat, he resigned himself to accepting her charity.

"I realize my actions tonight come as a surprise," he began. "To both of us. The truth is, Miss Willis, I have admired you for quite some time. Years, even. But I did not understand the depth of my feelings for you until this evening. The only remedy for my agony is for us to marry as soon as humanly possible."

Only then could he take her to bed and relieve his nigh-unbearable need to strip her naked, taste every inch of her delicious skin, touch her the way he'd imagined doing for so many years. She wouldn't refuse him. Emma was sensible, if more prideful than warranted.

Emma crossed her arms over her chest. "Is this a joke, Ardennes?"

Trick question. "Please call me Max. I prefer it. And no, I am utterly serious."

Please say yes.

"Allow me to be clear," said Emma. "I will not marry you, or anyone else, unless it is for mutual affection and respect. You have demonstrated neither of those qualities toward me at any point in the course of our acquaintance."

"A kiss is not affection?"

Her cheeks turned rosy. "Apart from one single, unexpected kiss."

"I propose you permit me to further demonstrate my affections—" Max leaned forward.

"Absolutely not!"

He halted, bent forward with one elbow on his knee. The color staining her cheeks turned crimson as she recoiled. Not the effect he was going for.

"You don't even like me, Max. Whatever brought this on, I am certain you'll think better of it by morning. Whereas I shall have to contend with the repercussions of your behavior this evening."

Frustration felt like shattered glass in his chest. He *had* been ungracious. Perhaps he'd earned his nickname after all.

"Do you recall the first Christmas we brought you to Gracepoint?" The Ardennes country estate, where his had father preferred to live year-round.

Warily, she nodded. "The time you compared me to pudding? Yes. I remember it vividly. I am not often called stupid."

"I meant that you were sweet and soft."

"It did not come across that way at the time."

He blew out a breath. "I was trying to make you laugh."

"By teasing me."

"Yes. Instead, you turned all spiky at me like an affronted hedgehog."

Emma's lips twitched into a faint smile before flattening again.

"It was an unkind thing to say to a girl who was spending her first holiday season alone. Your teasing was so bad that I begged to return to school early, even though it was only the headmaster's family and me until the next term started."

Max rocked back on his heels, remembering. "I didn't think you'd take it as a personal insult."

Emma's eyebrow arched skeptically.

"I know I have spent the past six years sparring with you when I should have told you how I thought about you every hour of every day. Give me a chance to prove how much I care about you." Seeing her resistance waver, he leaned in closer and feathered his blunt fingertips along her jaw. Emma flinched slightly but didn't pull away. He wanted to kiss her again, but decided she probably wouldn't let him get away with it a second time.

"Two weeks. Give me fourteen days to prove things can

be different between us. By the end, you'll see how right we are for one another."

Emma blinked as if coming out of a daze. Her gaze dropped briefly to his lips, then back up to his eyes, then shyly away. Triumph surged through him. She would have let him kiss her, after all.

Let her initiate the next one. He could be patient. For a while. If he must.

He would win her heart. Max felt confident that this heady mix of hope and lust and fear affected her, too.

"If you cannot convince me that your affections are genuine, you'll grant me my inheritance? And you'll leave my mornings free of interference? I refuse to let you monopolize my time for two entire weeks. You're rarely awake before mid-morning anyway."

Max hesitated, then lifted his chin and agreed. He would do anything to win her trust.

CHAPTER 6

Max's unexpected proposal made finding work Emma's topmost priority. Under the pretext of shopping, she spent the morning inquiring after positions as a telegraph clerk and a bookkeeper. Finding no success with either—she was too inexperienced for the former and the latter wanted too many hours—her hopes were raised by the sight of a hand-written sign in the window of Kiefer's Fine Books.

Perfect. If she could convince them to hire her, she could use the excuse that she was a bibliophile to an obsessive degree. Max would never get suspicious, despite there being a well-stocked library at his opulent townhouse for her to raid. In fact, Emma had deliberately chosen books she thought would irritate her guardian.

If Max noticed, he said nothing about her taste in reading. Defiance wasn't as easy as she'd hoped, when he ignored her misbehavior.

"May I help you, Miss?"

"Emma Willis. I wish to inquire after employment."

The clerk's bushy eyebrows rose.

"There is a sign in the window offering a part-time position. I meet the listed qualifications. My facility with numbers is excellent. I am well-read in a variety of subjects. I can assist customers with appropriate literary recommendations. I am not above performing menial tasks such as light dusting and tidying up."

She knew she was babbling. Emma had never tried to find a job before. The school had kept her on after matriculation, in exchange for board and pin money.

The shop clerk eyed her skeptically. "Does your husband know you're looking for work?"

How grating, that she couldn't sell her own labor for a fair price without the permission of a man.

"I have no husband, Mr…"

"Gill. I manage the shop for my uncle, who owns it." The clerk rubbed his chin thoughtfully. There were streaks of gray threaded through his dark hair. She guessed he was in his mid-thirties. "I'll have to speak with my uncle about hiring a woman. He won't pay the full advertised wage."

"Why not?" she demanded indignantly. Emma knew why. She wanted him to state the reason out loud.

"You're not a man. I can't pay you a man's wage."

"Twelve shillings a week is hardly a man's wage."

Don't argue, Emma scolded herself. Her teeth clamped lightly on her tongue—an internal rebuke that came too late.

"True, which is why we haven't been able to fill the position. If you'll leave your contact details and references, Miss Willis, I shall send word if the owner approves."

"Thank you." Emma took her time, writing carefully so there could be no mistake. The address was far too grand, so she listed a vague description of her presence at a duke's townhouse that one could interpret as her being a servant, instead of an unwanted guest.

If His Gracelessness ever found out what she was doing, he would undoubtedly force her to stop. Therefore, Max must never know.

Once she had her independence, she would no longer need to rely upon other people's grudging generosity. She wouldn't be a burden to anyone, ever again.

When she was done, she handed the sheet to the clerk and said, "I shall check back in a week if I haven't heard from you."

"There's no need, Miss Willis. I'll send word if we can offer you the position."

Emma held her head high as she exited the shop, even as she imagined her application being deposited into the wastebin.

·❧·

MAX STOOD when she entered the dining room at Ardennes House for lunch. Her heart skipped a beat at the sight of him dressed in shirtsleeves and a waistcoat. No jacket.

"Where were you this morning, Miss Willis—"

She raised one finger.

"We agreed. My mornings are mine to do with as I please. I am not obligated to report my whereabouts to you."

His lips parted as if to protest. She suddenly remembered the feeling of them pressed to her own. Flutters in her stomach. Still, Emma held her ground. Max's mouth flattened fractionally before he tipped his head to one side, indicating concession.

"What adventure do you have planned for us today, Miss Willis, that requires such a hearty meal?" He held out a dish of fresh fruit and scooped several spoonfuls onto her plate. Apparently, His Grace didn't mind her eating like a glutton. Emma was famished after rushing around all morning on her secret mission to find a job.

"I wish to compete in a regatta," she declared, around a mouthful of ham and cheese sandwich. "Do you happen to know any boaters?"

"As in, rowing?"

"Yes." She sighed. "All those strong men, pulling in unison. Not to mention those shirts they wear."

Max choked.

"Henley. The shirt is called a Henley." He sat straighter. "It's early in the season yet. Regattas aren't held until July. I do have a few chums from my school days who maintain their boating club access for practice. I suppose I could call in a favor. Are there any other unfeminine pursuits you'd like to experience?"

"Polo," Emma said. She might as well use the opportunity to try as many things as possible while he was feeling indulgent. "I wouldn't mind trying my hand at gambling, although I couldn't afford to lose any money. You'd have to bankroll me."

"And here I was hoping you might settle for riding astride." He sighed. "I should've known you'd choose outlandish activities."

"Do you think I could?" she asked with interest. "Ride astride?"

"You'll have to if you're serious about learning to play polo."

Emma *hmmed* thoughtfully. "What about a horse race?"

"We can race in Hyde Park if you give up your secret morning activity."

"Not like that, Max. I want to race on a proper track."

"I admit, that does sound interesting."

"Does that mean you've never tried it before?"

"Of course not. I cannot risk my neck before I've

secured an heir. I refuse to be the man who breaks eight generations of primogeniture."

"You anticipate becoming a father, then," Emma asked. A piece of ham lodged uncomfortably in her throat.

"It is expected of a duke."

"Yes, but you're more than a duke. You're also a man."

When Emma lifted her gaze to his, sparks might as well have flashed at the contact.

"You noticed."

Heat steamed her face.

"Finish up, darling. Before I can take you boating, you have an appointment."

"I do?"

"Remember my instructions to Adkins and Pindell yesterday evening?"

"To visit at half-past two if their intentions were sincere?"

"Indeed."

"But you said..." she trailed off in confusion. A shiver worked down her spine at the memory of his growled, *You're not marrying anyone but me.*

"I know what I said, Emma. They, however, do not." He held out one hand. "Come. Let's disabuse Pindell of any notion that he'll ever lay a hand on your delectable person."

Emma made a face. "And you think you will?"

Max's self-assured half-grin twisted her insides. Feelings were stupid things. She wasn't letting him seduce her this easily. He'd switched from antagonism to charm, and he could switch right back again at any time.

"The way you look at me, Emma, tells me you've wanted me as badly as I did you all these years. You're as eager for me to touch you as I am to oblige you."

She snorted in derision, but Emma was afraid he might be right.

CHAPTER 7

"I've never had to turn down a suitor before," Emma mused. "Never mind two offers in a single afternoon."

"Third proposal's the charm," Max said cheerfully. Thirteen days to win her heart. He ought to have begun years ago, instead of getting so flustered in Emma's presence that he parried her rapier wit with barbs of his own. They'd both been too proud to stand down.

Emma propped her chin on her hand and said, "What if I turn down the third proposal, too?"

"Then you're a fool."

Max let his mouth quirk up in a half-grin. She blushed and glanced away. "Honest question, Emma. Why wouldn't you want to be my duchess?"

"We both know I'm not fit for such a role," she hedged.

"If you're my wife, you're fit. Full stop." He unlocked the boat house doors. The odor of damp wood took him back to his university days. "A duchess defines her role. Not the other way around." Max found the device he was looking for and held it out. "Here. Put this on."

"What is it?"

"A life jacket. The interior is cork. I'll indulge your sense of adventure, but I won't risk your life, Emma. I assume you can't swim."

"Not well. Is that something we can add to our agenda?"

Her enthusiasm tugged his lips into a smile. She must have felt so stifled at that stuffy finishing school.

"Getting to Brighton and back would consume more time than we have allotted. I promise you, though, that if you want to learn how to swim, I shall find a way to make it happen." Max tightened the straps so the life jacket fit snugly around her torso. Perhaps he could prevail upon someone to use a private pool. They could swim without bathing costumes…

Possibilities whirled through his mind.

"Is the river cold this time of year?" Emma asked, interrupting his daydream of swimming naked with her.

"It's cold year-round. If you're not a strong swimmer and weighted down with skirts and shoes, this jacket could mean the difference between survival and drowning."

"I wasn't proposing to leave it off, Max. I want to try rowing, not die in the process."

Emma twirled to show off the awkward flotation device. Her skirt belled out. Everything between her waist and her shoulders was padded with cork-stuffed cotton twill. When she stopped spinning, she frowned.

"Where is your life jacket?"

"I don't need one. I'm a strong swimmer, and I'm not wearing a skirt." He stripped off his knit jersey and tossed it aside, standing in that shirt she liked so much. The Henley.

Emma rested her chin on her fist while her gaze skimmed down the row of buttons marching straight down his sternum. She caught herself staring and jerked her gaze away, saying, "Perhaps I ought to start wearing trousers, for ease of mobility."

Max's loins tightened. Heaven help them both if she adopted men's fashion. He wouldn't be able to keep his hands off her.

"We'll use this boat." He gestured to a low-slung shell tethered to the pier, stepped into the flat bottom and offered Emma his hand. She placed one delicate palm into his. Max's pulse quickened at the contact.

He rolled up his sleeves and placed the oars into the oarlocks. Emma perched on the bench opposite him. Even with his legs bent, his knees pressed into the fabric of her dress. She shifted away, her cheeks pinkening.

Max untied the rope from the cleat and deftly maneuvered them into the river's middle, where the current was stronger.

"May I try?"

Max had taken them into the center of the river where the water ran smoothest. He showed her how to grip the oars, then covered her gloved hands with his ungloved ones and demonstrated the circular motion used to paddle forward.

"Like this."

Emma glanced at him, then away, then back again. Her glossy brown hair was pinned up, but tendrils escaped and floated around her face. How had he ever thought her mousy? Her pale blue eyes sparkled with excitement. Her lips were the color of spring roses, and the bulky life jacket couldn't conceal the elegant line of her neck.

"May I ask you something?"

Emma inclined her head. "As long as it isn't a proposal. I have disappointed quite enough men for one day. It's a tiring business."

"I won't. Not yet, although you must admit this makes

for as romantic a setting as one could hope for. Sunset on the water. A gentle breeze. Bucolic scenery as far as the eye can see."

Emma yawned discreetly, dashing Max's hopes of using their close proximity as an excuse for a kiss.

"Am I boring you?"

"No!" Her brows arched in twin arcs of horror. "I've had a long and exciting day, that's all. I'm enjoying this experience very much."

"Where did you go this morning?"

Emma held up one finger. "We agreed. Mornings are my time to do as I wish without interference. You have my afternoons for thirteen more days." Seizing the oars, she rowed with vigor. "Let's see how fast we can make this boat go!"

※

"I HAD no idea you had such a sense of adventure," Max said once they'd locked up the boathouse and were sitting on the grassy bank to watch the fading sunset. The remains of their picnic were in the hamper a few feet away. He'd never experienced a quiet interlude with a woman that felt so intimate.

"Well, I haven't had much opportunity to explore my interests, have I?" Emma asked, shifting her balance onto one hip, propped up on one arm. With her free hand, she stifled a yawn. "Adventuring was frowned upon at Mrs. Quarrie's. I had to be on my best behavior, lest I lose my place."

"You could have come to Gracepoint. No one forced you to return to the school."

Except…hadn't he?

Max sat straighter, kicking his long legs out and leaning back on his hands. Their shoulders brushed. Emma didn't move away.

"Looking back, I can understand how that might not have been an appealing option for you," he said after a few moments.

"I don't like feeling unwanted. Or useless."

"Did I make you feel that way?" Max's heart sank. Emma shrugged.

"I'd have stayed out of your way if you'd given me something productive to do."

"Like what?"

"I don't know. Anything."

"You're my ward, not my servant. When you're my wife, you won't need to lift a finger."

He dared to drop a kiss on the top of her head. Emma's sleek dark hair was warm from the fading sun, her hat unpinned and set aside.

"That's what I'm afraid of."

Confounding woman.

"Tell me. What would you do with your inheritance if you had the entire sum right now? Spend it all on hats and horse racing?"

Emma rolled her eyes. "As implausible as it may seem to a man who's incapable of dressing himself without assistance from a valet, my needs are modest. My inheritance is more than sufficient to secure safe housing and, when combined with satisfactory employment—"

"You cannot intend to *work*," he interjected, aghast. "For *money*."

"What do you have against honest labor?"

"You're a lady, Emma. Ladies do not work. I forbid it. Besides," he bent to whisper, "I intend to occupy all your time." Max plucked the last strawberry and touched it to her lips.

Emma brushed his hand away, so he popped the fruit into his own mouth instead. "What if I want to work?"

Max chortled. "You can't mean it. Why would anyone engage in toil if they could avoid it?"

"Because not everyone is a lazy snob like you?" Emma said sweetly, although he detected an implacable edge beneath her syrupy tone.

"Such a Puritan ethic." He clucked his tongue. "Unnecessary, dearest Emma. Nothing but the finest things in life for the mother of my children."

His comment made her turn away and blush prettily. He'd flustered her.

"Then I shall step aside while ladies stampede to volunteer for the position."

"Even my Henley isn't enticement enough?" He clutched his chest, miming a wound. Emma laughed.

"The shirt was a blatant excuse to display your manly assets, and you know it."

"Did it work?"

She swatted his arm instead of answering, then leaned her head on his shoulder. Max's heart swelled. A similar sensation visibly tented his trousers. He couldn't tell whether she noticed. Did Emma know what effect she had on him?

After a few minutes, her slight weight turned heavy. His wrists ached. His cock, too, for different reasons. He slipped one arm around her waist. Emma listed forward, and for one heart-stopping moment, he thought she was going to kiss him. Then she toppled, boneless, and Max had to scramble to catch her.

"Asleep," he mused ruefully. "I suppose this truly was a taxing day for you."

With his free hand, he scooped his arm beneath her knees and carefully rose to his feet. Emma's head rested against his shoulder, her arms crossed over her stomach, her lips gently parted. In this fashion, he carried her to his coach and set her on his lap. Max held her for the entire ride back to his townhouse.

CHAPTER 8

Emma awoke slowly, to the unfamiliar but delicious feeling of a person lying next to her. Being held felt so nice…

She froze, too shocked to breathe.

Max.

What was he doing in her bed?

"What time is it?" she gasped. The clock read a quarter to eight. She sagged with relief. There was plenty of time for her to go inquire after employment.

Yet that did not explain why Max was sleeping in her room. Nor did it present a solution for getting him out of there before they were caught together.

Emma rummaged her memories of last night and concluded that nothing untoward had happened, despite how good he'd looked in that Henley shirt with the sleeves rolled up.

Briefly, she wondered what it would be like to live knowing she could wake up in the same bed every morning for the rest of her life.

"You're awake early," Max said in a rough voice, startling her.

"It's late, actually. I'm usually up with the sun."

"Mmm. You'll have to become accustomed to sleeping in once we're married."

"We're not getting married, Max."

"Yesterday wasn't enough to convince you? I shall have to try harder today."

He tugged her close to his front, his arm draped over her waist. Even fully clothed, the bulge of his erection pressed against her bottom. She must be dreaming. Emma interwove her unsteady fingers with his and wondered what the protocol was for signaling, *please touch me.*

Helpfully, Max read her mind. His thumb brushed the underside of her breast.

"Did you remove my corset?" she asked in a voice throatier than normal. She didn't recognize herself. Needing things she didn't know how to articulate. Max had awakened a part of her Emma had spent the entirety of her adulthood ignoring, and now her body clamored for his touch.

"Someone had to. Why?"

He nuzzled her nape. The scrape of his stubble reverberated pleasantly through her body. An insistent ache settled between her legs. Impatient with his slow teasing, she craned her neck for a kiss and at the same time guided his palm down her abdomen.

Max needed no further encouragement. He rolled her to her back, laying half on top of her as he palmed her breast through her chemise. Her petticoat and pantalets were twisted around her waist. Greedily, Emma cupped his face and opened to his deepening kiss. His weight pressed her into the bedclothes. His cock pressed insistently against the apex of her thighs. Experimentally, Emma tilted her hips fractionally upward and was rewarded with a grunt of surprise.

"Your curiosity extends beyond rowboats," he murmured. "Shall I indulge you, my sweet?"

Emma nodded. She skimmed her hands up his back, delighting in the play of muscle beneath the thin cotton of his Henley shirt. He'd not taken it off. Daringly, she tugged the hem up just far enough to glide the tips of her fingers along the bare skin above his waistband.

Propping himself on his elbows, Max reached behind his head and tugged the garment up and off. It should have been an awkward move, but he performed it so smoothly she couldn't help but imagine he'd practiced it hundreds of times, with hundreds of other women.

Well, if he could experience lovemaking without commitment, so could she. Her reputation was already in tatters after his outburst, and she didn't care what people in his social circle thought of her anyway. Less than two weeks from now, she would be an independent woman—and Max would be on to his next conquest.

The sad thought scattered when he sat back, indicating she should take off her chemise. Shyly, Emma crossed her arms over her chest.

"Let me see you," he pleaded. She wanted the exhilaration of her first experience to be with him. For years, even in her deepest moments of loathing, part of her had yearned for him to see her as a woman instead of a girl. Emma was helpless against the desire burning in his eyes.

Part of her—most of her, if she was being honest—actually liked him. When he wasn't being a pompous arse, Max was a lot of fun to be around. If they'd been born as different people, they might have sparked in a different way.

Emma huffed and crossed over her chest, torn between

embarrassment and wanting to please him. Wanting to please Max was a novel experience, to be sure. She didn't entirely trust him not to laugh at her modest bosom.

"Go on," he said encouragingly.

With trembling hands, she slipped shell buttons at her bodice free and pulled the fabric over her head.

The sound he made at the sight of her bare breasts broke all remnants of her resistance.

"Beautiful," he said wonderingly.

"It's nothing you haven't seen before."

"I've never seen *you* like this before."

"No one has. Besides, I'm sure I can't measure up to all your courtesans and paramours."

"You vastly overestimate my interest in other women." Gently, he moved her hands away, holding her by the wrists as he looked his fill. "Ladies making themselves available made the chase rather boring. You, by contrast, were always off-limits, first by my father's orders, then due to my own clumsy attempts to treat you like a little sister, when what I felt toward you was anything but sisterly."

"It's too early for revelations, Max."

"Weren't you claiming to be a lark just minutes ago?"

She couldn't help but laugh.

He released her arms and skimmed calloused palms up her ribs, squeezing her breasts before he moved forward, pressing her into the bedclothes with his weight, his breath hot at her neck. Emma writhed against him, trying to take it all in: the heat of his kisses at her throat, the rough scrape of his hands on her sensitized skin, the feel of his body on hers. Nothing she'd imagined in her most feverish dreams compared to the reality of being with him.

"You're so soft," he murmured against her skin. Emma didn't feel soft; her body felt wanton and desperate, needing him in places he hadn't yet explored.

Yet she wanted to draw this out, too. The feeling of him on her. The intimacy.

"You…aren't." She worked one hand between their bodies to squeeze his cock lightly. "Quite the opposite."

"If only you knew how often your presence puts me in this condition. It has been the most vexing thing to want you so badly, despite your constant abuse—" He nuzzled her neck. Emma giggled.

"I wasn't that bad!"

"I have never been likened to a turnip before."

"Nor I to a pudding." Relenting, Emma added, "Perhaps I was too eager to take you down a peg."

"Finally, she admits it."

Her grin wavered.

"I cannot fathom why you, a handsome, titled, obscenely wealthy lord, would take the slightest interest in an illegitimate nobody like me."

If this was all an elaborate joke to humiliate and ruin her, Emma would change her name, move to the Continent, and never return to England again.

"I should never have said that. I'm sorry, darling." His expression darkened. He rucked her petticoat up far enough to get his hand beneath the layers of cotton and murmured, "What can I do to demonstrate my remorse?"

For once, Emma had no words. How alarming to realize she already believed his sincerity. It was written in the worshipful way he looked at her, in the slight unsteadiness of his hands as he touched her in ways she'd never imagined.

Max made quick work of the tiny buttons, hooks, and ribbons holding closed her petticoats and pantalettes. He stripped them down her hips, leaving her naked on the bed. He knelt between her thighs, his hot gaze snagging on her stomach as he skimmed down her body.

"You are the most beautiful woman I have ever seen."

He traced one finger up her center. Emma gasped. All thoughts evaporated from her head when he slid two digits inside her. Her fingers curled around his forearm, clenching in time with each stroke as he pumped in and out.

She hadn't known she needed this. Emma gave in, tilting to meet his rhythm. Little frantic wails burst out of her.

"Shh, someone will hear us."

Oh, God, everyone in the household would know where Max slept last night and what they were doing now. Emma couldn't bring herself to care. This was the biggest adventure she'd ever dared to imagine, and she wasn't about to back out of it now. She'd deal with the consequences later.

Even if it meant marrying Max.

He lay beside her, half on top of her, curling his fingers to hit a spot inside her that made Emma's back arch off the bed.

"Like that?" he growled.

She moaned against his shoulder. The climax hit hard, stiffening her muscles and dragging a low wail from her throat. Max grunted and delved deep, keeping a steady rhythm that drew out her pleasure for so long that it left her gasping when it finally subsided.

He chuckled with evident satisfaction and pressed a kiss to her forehead, then rolled away. His cock tented his trousers, visibly. Emma frowned. "Wait. What about you?"

"Another time, darling."

Emma lay there, stunned, while Max shrugged into his shirt and sneaked out of her room like a common thief. She never would have expected her arrogant duke to give pleasure so generously, and then deny himself the same.

Clearly, she had misjudged him.

Or had she?

CHAPTER 9

"*A-choo!*"

Emma's nose itched. It ached on the inside before each dust-induced sneeze. Had she known her first day at Kiefer's Fine Books would involve climbing onto step stools, balancing while she leaned out to reach the books at the end of the shelf, and bending down to get to the bottom row, she would not have had her maid lace her corset so tightly. Not that she exactly wore her lacings tight in the first place.

Worse, her new day dress was covered in gray smudges. As much as she resisted being too invested in clothing, she was dismayed to realize what she'd done to a brand-new dress. Though she'd never gone wanting, it was a rare treat to have nice things.

"Are you ill, Miss Willis?"

Mr. Gill hovered nervously nearby, his spectacles slipping down the bridge of his narrow nose. He poked them back up.

"The dust is getting to me," she confessed. "I might step outside for some air—"

"No breaks are permitted, I'm afraid. You work such a short shift. I would have to dock your pay for the time."

Emma scratched the side of her nose and sighed. She'd been so excited to start her new position that she'd arrived half an hour before opening, but there had been no mention of additional pay for her time, then.

She wasn't sure what to do about the owner's request for written permission to work from her father (impossible, as he was deceased). Admitting she was the ward of a prominent duke was out of the question. Yet, if she did not produce a signed letter of approval from her male guardian, she would not be able to continue working.

Emma knew how that conversation would go.

Max, I'd like to work in a bookshop.

Emma, be serious.

I am serious.

Commence exaggerated sighs followed by an outright refusal.

Max would never understand her reasons for wanting to work. Her pin money could be revoked. Her meager savings from teaching at the school weren't sufficient to secure housing for more than a month or two. Without funds, she would be forever dependent upon people who were indifferent to her welfare.

A duke never had to learn the hard lesson that obligation bred resentment.

Her mother never wanted her in the first place, depositing her with Emma's grandmother as soon as she was weaned. Gran turned increasingly resentful of having to raise a child in her declining years—despite it being Emma who did most of the chores.

Her father had promptly shipped her off to a cold, rigid finishing school without bothering to meet her first. Emma carved out a place for herself through diligent study, but she never made many friends. She'd only stayed on because she had nowhere else to go except Gracepoint, where there was nothing for her to do but rattle around trying to avoid its owner.

If she wasn't useful, no one wanted her around.

And there was no way for her to be useful to a duke.

Max had a dizzying number of servants in his employ. She could hardly turn without tripping over a maid offering to relieve her of a shawl, or assist her with a trivial task. He did not need her.

Kiefer's Fine Books did. Even if it was only to dust tomes that obviously hadn't been touched by a customer in months.

"Mr. Gill," she ventured. "Have you considered placing some of these books on a shelf out front for a reduced price?"

"No. Why on earth would I do that?" he asked absently, poring over the sales ledger.

"To attract customers passing by the shop."

He glanced up.

"They might stop to browse the books, and come inside to purchase one. You'll have a better opportunity to show them more expensive options than if they never come into the store at all."

"But I'd have to reduce the price on the ones I put out. They might get stolen or damaged."

"They aren't doing much for the shop down here gathering dust, now, are they?"

"A sensible suggestion, Miss Willis. I shall speak with my uncle and perhaps give it a try."

Pleased, Emma finished her shift and hurried home just in time to change her soiled dress before meeting Max for lunch.

Emma eyed the ball she was meant to hit where it lay on the bright green field and hefted the rubber mallet with which she was meant to do it. Her horse shifted beneath her. Polo seemed like a simple enough sport from the ground. Ride a horse around a field. Hit the ball in the direction of the net. Hope it goes in. Repeat until it does or your team loses.

Perhaps it was a simple game for accomplished equestrians. Emma was not remotely accomplished. She nudged her bay mare's sides.

"Give her a solid kick!"

Emma tried. The horse trotted a short distance, then halted. She lost her grip on the mallet. Again.

"Better," Max called out. He, of course, was maddeningly competent at getting recalcitrant herbivores to do his bidding.

"I can't do this!" Her wail ended in a giggle, though. "I've been trying all afternoon, yet my horse has barely traveled halfway down the field. She just wants to eat grass." Emma patted the mare's neck. "Some polo pony you are."

"She's a fine pony. Gentle temperament. You're not being firm enough with her."

"I don't want to hurt her."

"You won't."

Max held out the mallet she'd dropped, but Emma shook her head. "I'm getting down."

Her legs didn't work properly. She had, in fact, donned trousers for this excursion. It felt strange to be out in public dressed so scandalously. She'd attracted more than a few second looks.

Her foot wouldn't come free of the stirrup. Max caught

her by the waist while she kicked free, sliding her brazenly down his chest, and he didn't let go once her feet were securely on the grass.

"Steady on."

"You can let go now."

Max chuckled. She didn't want to acknowledge the pang of loss when his hands slipped away from her hips.

Each morning for the past week, she'd awakened early to his sleeping form curled around hers. She'd fallen asleep after every single outing. Between the exertion of her job at Kiefer's and the busy afternoons Max planned for her, which on several occasions extended into the night, she kept dozing off during the coach rides home. He would carry her to her room, remove her outer garments and corset, and climb into the narrow bed wearing his trousers and undershirt.

Scandalous.

She knew he was doing it, at least in part, because he expected her to say yes to his upcoming marriage proposal. Any whispers of impropriety would be papered over by their subsequent nuptials. Despite this, Max was always careful to slip out of her room and return to his own chambers before her maid arrived with Emma's breakfast tray.

In between, they kissed and touched and talked, laughing about their adventures of the day before and dreaming up new ones.

Imagine waking up like that every day for the rest of your life.

She could. All too well.

Emma had never been so happy. She didn't trust this feeling. He was a duke. There would be nothing to stop him from seeking out a paramour once he tired of spending time with his mousy little ward.

She was still an *illegitimate nobody,* even if he'd apologized for saying that to her face.

A week ago, she'd been certain they wouldn't make it through their negotiated courtship period without murdering one another. Now, Emma was starting to worry she wouldn't be able to muster the courage to resist him once the week was up.

"Are you ready to watch a real game?" He took the reins to lead her recalcitrant pony off the field.

"I can't keep abusing this poor animal." Emma winced with each step. The first time she'd tried riding astride was two days ago, during their race at a private track where one of Max's fancy friends bred thoroughbreds. He'd let her win. Twice. She'd thought the soreness would fade, but if anything, it was worse two days later.

She changed into a skirt and returned to the field, where eight men on horseback had assembled. They wore colored uniforms to indicate who belonged to which team.

All of this was new to her. Polo was not an activity she'd ever had an opportunity to participate in, even as a spectator.

After each seven-minute playing period, or chukka, the players changed horses. He played in the third position, which, he'd explained with evident pride, was the most demanding role.

Her gaze flicked to his tall, broad form. His horse was necessarily the largest, which put him at a disadvantage when it came to making quick turns. He had to anticipate the other players and guide his mount accordingly by making split-second decisions. Emma couldn't ignore the flutter in her midsection every time he scored a goal and flashed her a grin.

At the midpoint of the game, she and other spectators were invited onto the field to push divots of grass back into place. Max, breathing hard, strode over to her.

"Are you enjoying the spectacle?"

"Very much. You're an excellent player." Self-consciously, she examined the sod and toed another clump of grass into place. "I see now why I struggled to manage the horse and the mallet. You make it look easy, but it's quite a trick to put it all together."

"Tiring, too. I've reserved places for us to eat supper at the clubhouse dining room this evening. I may be the one who falls asleep during the ride home tonight."

She sensed his hesitation. He wanted to ask where she spent her mornings. But Emma wasn't going to tell him. Working at the bookshop was a much-needed reminder that she was not, in fact, a future duchess. This interlude would end, and soon.

The more she could keep that fact foremost in her mind, the less it would hurt to let go.

Or so she hoped.

"I believe that's your signal," she said. To her great surprise, Max bent to press a quick kiss to her lips before striding away.

CHAPTER 10

That night, they both fell asleep during the ride home. Emma, as usual, nodded off first, with her head on his shoulder. Max scooped her in close, and before he knew it, he was jolted awake by the footman putting down the step.

Emma barely stirred when he scooped her up and carried her into the house.

What the devil was she doing every morning?

He was half inclined to follow her, but that would be an invasion of her privacy. He was trying very hard to earn her trust after having spent years undermining it with sarcasm and insults, and he felt certain his efforts were working. He could restrain his curiosity for a few more days.

Max laid her on the bed, carefully undid her buttons, and wrestled the confounded corset off without waking her. This time, he went one step further than usual and removed everything except her chemise. Then he stripped down to his underwear and crawled under the covers beside her.

So much better than wearing his trousers to bed.

With less fabric between their bodies, a new problem

presented itself the next morning. Pale light filtered in through the drapes he'd yet again forgotten to close. Max slowly registered the warm weight of a sleeping woman, her back tucked fully against his front. His erection nestled beneath her delectable arse. With any other woman, he would rouse her with kisses to the nape of her neck, and after a decent amount of foreplay, hike up her chemise and slide inside her.

But this was Emma.

Innocent, prickly, wary Emma. He'd been slowly introducing her to the delights of the flesh each morning. It required every ounce of his willpower to walk away unsatisfied each morning.

Removing his clothing had been a mistake.

Her calves whispered against his legs. He stroked the underside of her breast. Emma stirred.

He waited with bated breath.

Emma squirmed and covered his hand with her warm, soft, small one.

To his utter delight—and a rush of blood to his loins—she pushed his hand down.

"Stop teasing me and get on with it," she ordered. Apparently, she'd been more awake than he thought.

Max rocked his erection against her bottom, rucking up her hem and finding her slick with desire. He sank two fingers inside her and began a steady stroking. Emma rocked with him, her pants turning into moans.

He wasn't going to be able to summon the will to walk away. Not today.

Her back stiffened. Max smiled into her hair and worked her until his hand ached, reveling as he took her through the climax. "That's it, sweetheart. Come for me."

She pulsed around him, panting wordlessly, her hand clamped around his forearm. He would never think of forearms the same way again, after the way she'd stared and squirmed when he rolled up his sleeves in the rowing shell, and now the way she clutched at him in mindless desperation.

What was he going to do about his own torrid state?

Max pondered his options for returning to his own quarters while sporting a raging erection, without embarrassment, and quickly concluded there weren't any good ones. Even the most discreet servants whispered about the scandal of a grown man and his grown but legally dependent ward sharing a bed every night.

Beside him, Emma twisted. She sat up, her luscious hair tangled and eyes bright. To his shock and delight, she straddled his thighs and said, "It's my turn to try pleasuring you."

Heaven help him, Max couldn't bring himself to refuse.

CHAPTER 11

Emma stared at the swell of Max's cock beneath his linen drawers. The close-fitting garment delineated the heavy round base and tented at a slight angle toward his left hip bone. Muscles honed by rowing and riding rippled upward along his stomach. Above that expanse, she found defined pectorals dusted with dark hair, dotted with flat nipples. Farther up, his sharp clavicles framed a strong throat leading to a chiseled chin and sensuous lips.

She inhaled, steeling herself to meet his eyes. What if he didn't want to be the recipient of her fumbling first attempt to pleasure a man?

Max's gaze bore into hers. Thank goodness it was still dim in her room. She wasn't sure she could withstand the intensity of his unfettered emotions in the full light of day.

"Go on," he said in a rough voice.

Experimentally, she traced the shape of his cock. It was longer than her hand, and appeared far too big to fit in her mouth—never mind elsewhere. Still. She had the strange impulse to try licking it, so she unfastened the button holding his drawers closed and skimmed them down his narrow hips. He shifted to help her.

"Is this alright?" she asked, running the tip of her finger down the underside.

"More," he ground out. "Touch me like this."

He demonstrated, covering her hand with his large one. Her fingers couldn't quite close around him. Max showed her how to move up and down. A single droplet beaded on the slit at the center of the rounded head. Fascinated, she scooted back and ran her tongue over it.

Max's abdomen rippled. He covered his face with both hands and groaned.

"Should I stop?"

"God, no. Do that more."

Ah, she was starting to understand now. He liked it when she touched him with confidence.

Apparently, he wasn't put off by her inexperience, so Emma spent the next several minutes discovering what made his abdomen do that fascinating ripple again. He liked it when she ran firm strokes up and down his shaft. It happened again when she gently squeezed the heavy orb at his base, too. When she opened her mouth wide and took him inside that way, his stomach muscles tensed gratifyingly and Max spiked his hands into her hair with a low groan.

This was going so well, she decided it was time to take things further.

She released him, her jaw aching, and slid upward along his torso. To her astonishment, Max drew her to him and kissed her hungrily. Pleasuring him with her mouth hadn't put him off from kissing her. She had so much to learn, and he was an unexpectedly patient instructor.

Until the moment he flipped her onto her back and kissed his way down to her breasts, palming one and sucking the other into his hot mouth. He'd done this twice before. The first time, the shock had been so intense she'd shoved him away. The second time, she'd moaned and clutched him to her, seeking more, until Max had been the one to stop, panting raggedly as he pulled on his clothing and made a hasty departure. He left her there, confused about what she'd done wrong and stewing in her own want.

Would he do the same thing this time?

No. Instead, he continued kissing his way down her stomach and draped her leg over one shoulder, leaving her exposed and breathless with anticipation.

Surely, he wouldn't…

Max bent his head and licked her.

Emma gasped.

Correctly interpreting this as encouragement, he spread her open and kept licking her until she couldn't hold still. Meaningless sounds bubbled out of her. Tension built within her core. So close.

"Like this, sweetheart?"

She could only nod. His chuckle tickled her sensitive thighs. He nipped her there, a startling counterpoint to the glide of his tongue through her wet folds. She yelped, then exhaled raggedly when he continued to suck her most sensitive place.

When he'd driven her to the brink, Max thrust his fingers inside her and bore down on the sensitive nub with the flat of his tongue, sending her hurtling blindly through the climax.

Slowly, Emma's eyes fluttered open. Max was crawling up her body, his cock rampant at her hip.

"We should stop here."

She shook her head, hair sliding along the pillowcase.

"I want to do this with you."

His eyes darkened. She held her breath.

"What about our wedding night?"

For the first time, she seriously considered saying yes at the end of their two weeks. If that was the only way he'd finish this, instead of taking her over the precipice again and again, in every conceivable way but the expected one, so be it. She'd marry him and deal with the consequences later.

But Emma wasn't ready to capitulate quite yet.

"What about it?" she countered. "We'd still have one. It would still be our first time together as a married couple."

If they married.

"You won't regret it not being special?"

"It would still be special," she insisted. "Besides, what if we aren't compatible that way? Wouldn't you rather know before we make things permanent?"

"Not…compatible?" he said with evident confusion.

"You are very large. I am not."

As she said this, Emma hooked one leg around the backs of his thighs. It wouldn't take very much. A slight shift of his hips, alignment, a single thrust, and her aching curiosity would be satisfied. Perhaps painfully.

Max's shoulders shook with his chuckle.

"You know how to break a man's resistance."

She grinned. "I'm not sensing much resistance, Max."

He kissed her. She tasted herself on his lips. It wasn't bad at all. In fact, the intimacy of that kiss sent a thrill through her. The unfamiliar stroke of his head against her sex heightened her anticipation. A strange pressure, a pinch of pain, and then a fullness the likes of which she'd never experienced before. Emma gasped and clutched him. Max grunted.

"I love the way you do that."

"Do what?"

"Cling to me. Whatever you can grab onto." He brushed

a kiss against her temple, cradling her in his arms. "Are you alright?"

She'd never felt so treasured.

"Mmm. Fine. This is nice, but surely this isn't all there is to the process?"

His helpless chuckle rumbled through his chest. Emma instantly regretted teasing him, for he slipped out. A protest rose to her lips, but before she could give it voice, he thrust again, and it became a mindless gasp of *yes*.

This was so much better than she'd imagined. Max repeated the process, still slow, still gentle, even as he picked up speed. Emma's thighs twinged. Between riding a polo pony and now him, muscles she'd never been aware of before were complaining loudly of soreness.

No matter. She wouldn't stop this for the world.

"Emma," he muttered through clenched teeth. "Emma, you don't know how badly I've wanted you."

She did, though. She'd wanted him the same way, though her pride wouldn't let her admit it, even to herself. Emma gripped his hips between her thighs, tensing in anticipation of the oncoming climax. She could feel it building with each stroke. The wet, rhythmic slapping sound of his body on hers echoed in her ears.

When it hit, she grabbed his buttocks as if to drive him as deep inside her as he could go. Max's rhythm broke as she shattered around him. He ground out her name through clenched teeth, followed by a litany of filthy words.

"Emma. Emma. Fuck, Emma. Fuck, you're so good, so tight, so perfect. It feels so good to be inside you. You like coming on my cock, don't you, my sweet girl."

Boneless and trembling, Emma inhaled the scent of his skin, memorizing the moment. Yes, she would marry for this.

But would it be like this ever again? Or was it only because it was her first time that it had been so intense?

Max rolled onto his back, threw one arm over his eyes, and tucked her close to his body. Emma pushed up onto her elbow. "Aren't you going to leave?"

"Do you want me to?"

"No. I'd rather you stayed."

He grinned and pulled her onto his chest. Together, they again fell fast asleep.

CHAPTER 12

Hours later, dressed in a plain gray wool dress, Emma burst into the bookshop. The tattletale bell over the door loudly announced her late arrival.

"Miss Willis. You're eight minutes tardy."

Mr. Gill snapped his pocket watch closed.

"I do apologize, sir. I was delayed by traffic."

"I expect promptness. I shall have to dock your pay by a quarter-hour."

"But I'm only eight minutes late!" Emma tied the apron around her waist and tucked a dusting rag into the pocket.

"Had you been seven minutes late, I would have rounded down and paid you. Since you were delayed more than halfway through the quarter hour, I am obligated in the name of fairness to dock your pay for the full fifteen minutes. If you ensure you are on time in the future, you will not suffer the consequences of lateness. Understood?"

"Understood."

Fairness, Emma wondered, to whom?

She set about updating the display in the window. The

books' covers had faded with sun exposure, so she put them on the cart to sell at a discount.

"Not this one, Miss Willis." Mr. Gill selected one volume. "Don't you recognize a rare edition when you see one? It's too valuable to risk putting it outside."

"Personally, I wouldn't have placed it in the window where it could be sun damaged."

He squinted at her over the rims of his spectacles and sighed. Emma held her breath, expecting to be let go for her impertinence. Why couldn't she curb her tongue?

"We're fortunate to have your keen eye." The shop clerk gave her a rare smile. "Why don't you try putting together a display to attract more customers?"

Emma's eyes watered, and not because of all the dust. In spite of his grumpiness and her outspokenness, here, she was wanted. Needed. And she intended to create the best bookshop window the world had ever seen.

꒰ ꒱

DESIGNING the new display took several mornings of work, between scrubbing the glass until it sparkled and creating paper cutouts of characters from children's stories. There was a white rabbit and a little girl in a blue dress, and a boy with a top hat and gold foil coins to advertise Pip from *Great Expectations*.

"Fanciful," Mr. Gill commented, eyeing her handiwork. "Miss Willis, you have not yet returned your signed permission for employment. I am afraid I cannot pay you for your labor until you've done so."

Emma's heart sank. She couldn't ask Max to sign it. He would demand that she quit. She might not need this job for the paltry pay, but she needed it for her pride. It would be so easy to become accustomed to the luxury Max took for granted—and difficult to adjust her expectations once she no longer had access to it.

Nothing in life was permanent. She'd learned that lesson long ago. Best to keep her expectations in line with her likely future.

This job was a stepping stone to whatever would get her through the next bout of turmoil that would inevitably upend her life. She could not lose it.

Which meant one thing: she must forge a man's signature to grant herself permission to work. Ideally, Max's notoriously recognizable scrawl. If only she hadn't burned every single letter he'd sent, immediately after reading it, she would have had an example to copy.

She sighed. As long as it didn't look like her own feminine script, it would be believable. But revealing her guardian's identity posed an entirely different set of problems.

Emma didn't like to lie. In this case, she didn't have a choice.

~

Maximus Aloysius Tremaine
Maximus A. Tremaine
M.A. Tremaine

Emma threw down her pen. Even her punctuation looked like a woman's writing. Neat, curving, precise.

Making up a story wholesale on the fly would only expose her as a liar. She needed to stay as close to the truth as possible without revealing her guardian's identity.

"Emma?"

She hastily shoved the papers under a stack.

"There you are. I thought you were resting?"

Was it her imagination, or was there a suggestive undertone to his question? Emma's stomach fluttered. She was tired, but too anxious to sleep. Tonight, Max wanted to take her to an actual ball, filled with aristocrats like him.

That meant close physical proximity with him on a public dance floor. Everyone would be watching her. Emma didn't trust herself not to trip over the hem of her own skirt, tread on his toes and spin in the wrong direction. Possibly in quick succession.

Emma could never be Max's duchess. His wife would be expected to be social and gracious, witty and confident under any circumstances. Not awkward and bluntly outspoken like she was. Literally any other woman on Earth would make a better duchess than an illegitimate nobody like her.

Her throat tightened at the thought of Max married to someone else.

"I was." Her mind whirled with excuses. "I couldn't rest, so I thought I'd write…"

"A letter?" he prompted.

"Yes!"

"To whom?"

Emma had no one. He knew full well she had few acquaintances from the school, all of whom had graduated, married, and no longer had time for their odd spinster friend. Her family was all dead.

"Never mind." Max raised both hands, palms outward. "It's not my affair. If you are awake, would you like to come with me to see an art exhibition? A friend of a friend of a friend's gallery is opening tomorrow at Kew." Wryly, he added, "I wouldn't otherwise consider going, but you might like the subject. Botanical prints and landscapes."

"Yes!" Emma leaped up, clapping her hands with delight. He was willing to associate his name with an artist he might not otherwise care for, simply because she might like it. "I'd love to meet him."

"Her," Max corrected, smiling. "Marianne North. She's quite the world traveler. I think you'd get along splendidly."

Her heart did a funny flop in her chest.

He wasn't supposed to be charming. Or thoughtful. Or fun.

Max was supposed to be an arrogant, insufferable arsehole. Sometimes, he still was. But ever since he'd put his mind to courting her, Emma didn't have a single complaint about him.

That made him dangerous. Max had the capacity to devastate her so deeply she would never recover from the loss. She could not afford to let that happen.

"What's this?"

She'd covered up her attempts to practice forgery, but Emma had left the damned request from Kiefer's Fine Books sitting out on her desk. Max picked it up and read it quickly.

"That's mine!"

Panic surged through her.

"Your debts are mine. If you owe money to a shop, I won't have you paying it out of your own funds." He frowned. "This is the secret you've been hiding? You're employed? In a bookstore?"

The amusement in his voice cut Emma to the quick.

"What's wrong with that, Max?"

"You're to be a duchess. My duchess. Why on earth would you want to tire yourself out lugging around dusty books, when you could have a life of leisure with me?"

Beneath his laughter, Emma heard a note of confusion. Her heart cracked.

He didn't get it. He did not understand her, even after all the time they'd spent together.

She'd trod on grass divots that had more insight than Maximus Assimus Tremaine.

Suddenly, Emma felt very alone in the world. It was a bitter reminder that she had no place in his life. He'd brought her here to get rid of her, after all. Courting her had been nothing but one of his temporary whims.

"I cannot spend my days in idleness, Max, no matter how entertaining. I need to feel useful. If I'm not working, I don't…I'll be…"

She couldn't bring herself to say the word *worthless*.

"Free to entertain your husband?"

Max waggled his eyebrows, turning the moment into a joke. Except that nothing about this was funny to her.

Feelings faded. She would never be anything more than a rich man's unwanted daughter. Emma could not bear the thought of becoming another entitled rich man's equally unwanted wife. Especially his.

"I'm sorry, Max. I can't." The words stuck in her throat. "We had a nice time together. I shall treasure the memories."

"You don't mean…" He hesitated. "I see. I haven't changed your mind at all. You want me to sign this letter, write you a bank draft for the sum of your inheritance, and let you walk away."

Emma could only nod. It wasn't that she wanted it; she needed it. For her own sanity.

There was nothing more precious than independence.

"Very well."

Max strode to the desk, took up his pen and scrawled his name in florid script at the bottom of her drafted letter. Did he read the words she'd crafted so carefully in an attempt to sound like him, expressing her deepest desires?

He didn't bother to sit down. Tears stung her eyes. He wanted her gone as soon as humanly possible.

Their fingertips brushed when he passed her the papers. "I'll have your dowry transferred to a bank account in your name. Here is a hundred pounds to get you started. It is a gift. I know you'll manage your inheritance well, but it isn't a great deal of money. If you do find yourself in difficulty..." He inhaled. "Please be careful out there."

"My needs are simple, Max. I'm not used to all this." She gestured vaguely to their opulent surroundings. "I don't deserve such luxuries. I wouldn't have the slightest idea what to do, and we both know I can't hold my tongue. I'd be a disaster of a duchess."

He stroked her cheek fondly. "You'd be my defiant wife, and I'd adore every moment spent clashing with you," Max said wistfully. "But if this is what you want, little bird, then fly. I won't try to cage you anymore."

With that, Emma's heart shattered completely. She stood rooted to the spot as Max brushed past her, closing the door behind him with a soft click.

Only then did she let the tears fall.

Her worst suspicions had been correct. He'd never truly wanted her. Not enough to fight for her. It was time for her to go.

Where, she didn't know.

CHAPTER 13

The second morning she awoke alone in her musty bed, with an aching back from where the springs sagged in the middle, Emma truly regretted her decision to leave Max.

At Ardennes House, she could have had a permanent bed, instead of renting this inferior, temporary one.

She'd been a fool to turn down such luxury. Soft cotton sheets wound around Max's naked torso—

Don't think about it.

If she focused on what she'd given up, Emma would lose the courage to continue moving toward what she needed. Yes, this was grim, but it wasn't forever.

She tugged on her woolen dress, fastening the skirt around her waist and buttoning the jacket to her throat. Smudges of dust still darkened the hem in places, where she'd attempted to clean it yesterday. Despite washing herself with a cloth and soap wetted with water from the chipped pitcher and basin, Emma felt as if a film of dirt clung to her skin.

A pang of longing for a hot bath whenever she wanted one caught her off-guard.

"To think, I could have been a duchess," she muttered, surveying her cramped room. "Yet, I chose this."

There was no time to rue what might have been.

Her throat closed around a tangle of emotions. Regret. Envy. Pride. Emma shook it off and bent to check that her money was well hidden below the loose floorboard she'd found the day she moved in, then went down to a disappointing breakfast of a single egg and stale bread. The ladies' boarding house was a respectable establishment, but no more comfortable than Mrs. Quarrie's had been.

"Good morning, Mr. Gill," she said with determined cheer upon entering the shop, dropping her umbrella into the holder.

"Morning, Miss Willis. Would you mind restocking the cart? Once the weather clears, we'll try putting it out again."

Emma took a steadying breath. If she must live with the consequences of her decision, she needed a higher wage to support herself.

"Now that I've demonstrated my reliability and value to the store, Mr. Gill, I was hoping for a wage increase. You see, my financial circumstances have changed, and I cannot make ends meet on three hours of work each day."

"The owner won't countenance it," he said without looking up from the ledger where he was reviewing the previous day's sales. "Moreover, the shop can't financially support a second full-time employee. Perhaps in a few months my uncle would consider it."

"But I know the trick of putting out this cart helped to boost our receipts," she protested. Not to mention how her clever window display had increased the number of curious customers drawn inside to browse. "I can prove it."

"Yes, but it isn't as though we're going to give you all the profits, Miss Willis." He placed his hat upon his head and thrust his arms into the sleeves of a weatherproof coat. "I am off to evaluate a collection. Some toff selling off his grandfather's library. I expect there to be a number of interesting rare books to acquire. I'll be back before your shift ends. If the weather clears, remember to put the cart outside."

The bell jingled merrily, a striking counterpart to Mr. Gill's dismissiveness.

Emma busied herself by taking the opportunity to examine the accounts book in her employer's absence. What she discovered made her see red.

"What a lying cheat!"

She slammed the leather-bound ledger closed. "An eight-per-cent average daily sales increase would more than pay for a few more hours each week. The greedy git."

If she were the Duchess of Ardennes, no one would dare to take advantage of her this way.

There was being useful, and there was being used. This was the latter.

Teaching hadn't been fulfilling, and dusting books was even less so. Mr. Gill didn't need her; anyone could wield a duster. The sense of belonging she'd felt while working here wasn't real.

Remembering Max's crestfallen confusion when she turned down his proposal brought tears to her eyes now. For years, she'd wanted him to notice her—but when he did, she panicked and ran away. Emma had been so dedicated to protecting herself from rejection that she'd inflicted the same pain on the man she...

...*loved*.

Emma would not cry. She was angry and aching and all she wanted to do was fling herself into Max's arms and hear him say, *Everything will be alright, darling.* She missed his teasing. He'd have cracked a joke about stingy shopkeepers and made the whole situation moot by buying the entire bookstore for her, purely out of spite.

Max supported her dreams, no matter how outlandish or expensive, yet she'd been too blind to see that he expressed his love lavishly. He was simply too shy to say it with words.

As soon as Mr. Gill returned, she would go find Max and tell him how sorry she was for being such a stubborn fool.

One o'clock came and went. Her stomach rumbled. The bell over the door rang only a handful of times. She recorded two modest sales. There simply weren't many people out shopping on a soggy spring day.

By midafternoon, Emma was so hungry she thought she might faint.

She found a board on a string with a clock painted on it, set the moveable hands to indicate she would return within a quarter-hour, and hung it in the window facing outward. There was a tea house across the street where she could procure a sandwich.

Outside, she realized she had no way to lock the shop. Tears scalded her eyelids. Cold rain dripped down the back of her neck. Emma had never been so hungry in her life, but she couldn't leave the store standing open and unguarded.

What was she going to do?

"Miss Willis?"

"Max?" Emma whirled. Sure enough, there was her beloved duke, striding down the street, a full head taller than any other man around. Unforgettable. Her heart skipped a beat.

"I wondered if I would find you here. I meant to come

earlier, but…" He trailed off, looking as if he was torn between scooping her into his arms and turning back the way he'd come. "I was unsure of my welcome."

"I am so happy to see you, Max," she said in a rush. He scooped her into his arms. "This business of making my way in the world is hard," she mumbled into his shoulder, breathing in the damp wool scent of his clothes. She didn't want to be alone. She wanted to be loved.

His chest moved in what had to be a chuckle.

"Don't laugh at me."

"I'm not."

"You are." But then again, so was she. Emma locked her arms around his waist and buried her face in his jacket to hide it. With a rueful sniffle, she said, "I'm ridiculous, Max. I've been so afraid that you would send me away that I chose to remove myself before you could reject me."

"Why would you think I'd send you anywhere, Em? Isn't marriage a rather permanent condition?"

"So was motherhood, in theory, yet my mum left me with my grandmother as soon as I was weaned. She needed the work, but she also didn't want a baby." She shrugged. "My father only took responsibility for me after I was orphaned and there was no one else to care for me. His pride wouldn't let him be the kind of man who let his by-blow go to the workhouse, but he didn't exactly want me. Nor did your father want me for his ward, and definitely not you."

His arms tightened around her.

"Not as a ward, darling." Max lowered his lips to hers in a gentle, reassuring kiss so soft and sweet that Emma melted. "As a woman, yes. From the very beginning, though you were too young when we initially met, and I was too stupid to understand what I felt for you then." Another kiss, this one sensual enough to curl her toes. "I didn't mean to chase you away, then or now. I love you. I came looking for you to tell you that, in hopes it might change your mind. I respect your decision, but I wasn't ready to give up and let you walk away that easily."

Emma sniffed. The world blurred. "Oh, Max. I was locking up the shop with every intention of coming home. Well, I admit I was going to get lunch first. I'm starving. I've missed you. I want to wake up in your arms every morning for the rest of my life—"

He cut her off with another kiss.

"Miss Willis! What the devil are you doing?"

She and Max turned to find Mr. Gill hastening up the street, his coattails flapping at his knees and an angry red tinge on his scowling face.

"This is why women make terrible employees! Such wanton behavior reflects poorly on the shop. What will people think?"

"Perhaps had you returned before my shift ended, as promised, I might not have felt compelled to close the shop and seek my long-overdue lunch!" Emma declared.

"Since when does kissing a strange man in broad daylight qualify as sustenance?"

"You misunderstand the situation, Mr…"

"Gill. I manage the store."

"A pleasure to meet you, Mr. Gill. You may address me as Lord Tremaine, Duke of Ardennes and you will address my future wife with the utmost respect."

"Duke?" He glanced nervously at Emma and gulped. "Wife?"

"I wish to receive the money I've earned and exit your employment immediately, Mr. Gill. While I have enjoyed working in a bookshop, I find a different future beckons. His Grace will be occupying all of my time for the foreseeable future."

She looped her arm through Max's elbow and smiled up at him. Max patted her arm.

"Perhaps you should start your own bookshop, my sweet." A shaft of sunlight cut across his face, highlighting his handsome features. The clouds overhead cleared, and a rainbow suddenly brightened the entire street. "Since we're already here, I propose we visit the modiste and have you fitted for a wedding gown. If you'll do me the honor of marrying me as soon as the banns can be posted."

"Yes, Max. But first, food!" Emma exclaimed, pressing her free hand over her stomach.

Max laughed.

"I know just the place."

They sauntered away, arm-in-arm, leaving Mr. Gill sputtering in outraged astonishment.

EPILOGUE

EMMA, THREE YEARS LATER

"Do you have a copy of *Alice's Adventures in Wonderland?*"

"Indeed, we do, Lady Pindell." Emma crooked her finger. "Emma's Literary Emporium carries all the classics, both educational and entertaining. That particular book sells quickly, which is probably why you didn't see it on the shelf. Let me check the stock room."

The lady in question followed her closely.

"Aren't you worried you'll spoil the children with entertainment, rather than emphasizing education?"

Emma whirled on her heel.

"No. I firmly believe that children learn best through storytelling. Have you ever listened to a young child? They are full of imagination and curiosity. If we can harness that to the dull mechanics of literacy, we shall raise generations of enthusiastic readers. After all, a child who never opens a book can't learn anything from its contents."

Mrs. Pindell's eyebrows rose. Emma tried to rein in her enthusiasm.

"Allow me to rephrase. If I did not believe books were

an enriching experience for children, I wouldn't have opened a bookshop dedicated to literature specifically for them. I could spend my time on any other pursuit I fancied, but this one is dear to my heart. For what it's worth, the Queen herself agrees with me."

Emma had never expected to become friendly with Victoria, but it turned out that Society was far more forgiving of her outspokenness than she'd ever dared to hope.

Across the noisy, crowded store, she spied her very tall husband as he chased after their very small, very quick, eighteen-month-old daughter.

"Samantha Tremaine, get back here, you scamp!"

A squeal of delight echoed through the room. Emma bent awkwardly to scoop up her daughter and bussed a kiss to her chubby cheeks. Samantha kicked her burgeoning stomach. Wincing, Emma handed the little girl off to her father.

"Oof. Getting kicked fore and aft is not nice."

"Sorry," he mumbled. "That one is going to run circles around the gents one day."

"And us."

"Your Grace, if you don't mind, I've a gift to choose and I'm in a hurry." Lady Pindell's lips twitched in an indulgent smile.

"Yes, of course. Mr. Gill will assist you."

Emma brought the expensively bound volume to the front counter, where she handed it to her former boss to ring up and wrap in paper. After his uncle's bookstore closed due to low sales, she'd leased the space and hired him to run her bookstore.

What she originally intended to be a charity shop partially supported by sales had succeeded beyond her wildest expectations. The dusty, dour leather volumes waiting futilely to find homes among aspiring erudites had been replaced with shelves full of colorful children's literature, toys, and an eclectic selection of books Emma happened to enjoy. Works by Jane Austen sat alongside more adventurous fare by Henrik Ibsen and Elizabeth Gaskell.

The combination of playful items for children and adults alike had proven to be a winning business. Even if Max were to go bankrupt tomorrow, Emma would still be able to support her family. Her work was a source of pride and purpose, and Max never complained about how much of her time it absorbed. If anything, he liked to embarrass her by bragging about her success.

Mostly, she left the day-to-day management to Gill, for she had more important priorities—such as keeping Samantha's wiggly little body from toppling off the counter where her father had placed her.

"No testing the gravity," she scolded.

"Only her papa's patience," Max grumbled affectionately. "Are you ready for lunch?"

"More than ready." She was always hungry during this stage of pregnancy, although she could rarely eat very much. "The afternoon clerk will be here at one to relieve you for your midday break."

Emma, having experienced the unfairness of poor management, ensured that she always had sufficient, well-paid staff to cover the store during its operating hours.

"Yes, Your Grace."

"And stop with the 'your grace' nonsense," she ordered, not that he would listen. Not once since her marriage had he failed to address her formally.

"I have found just the place," Max said with pride, tucking Samantha into the crook of his arm. "You'll love it.

Last time we were there, I believe you declared it the best ham sandwich in all of London."

Emma laughed. Max loved to tease her by making a reservation at the tea shop where she'd wolfed down her lunch that day after confronting Mr. Gill on the street. Every time he made this joke, she claimed it was the best she'd ever eaten, despite the fare being rather mediocre. Unexciting food served both of their stomachs better than finer dining whenever they were obliged to ride in the carriage.

He drew her close and kissed her brazenly, in full view of anyone who cared to look. She threaded her hands through his hair and smiled against his mouth when Max whispered, "And I shall have you for dessert."

※

See Max fulfill his fantasy of teaching Emma to swim—
claim your free bonus epilogue:
https://BookHip.com/XFKRFPV

※

Find more Carrie Lomax books at www.carrielomax.com

Try a free book:
Belladonna: A Virtue & Vice Prequel

ABOUT THE AUTHOR

Carrie Lomax is the bestselling author of historical & contemporary romance. She also writes angsty new adult fantasy romance under the pen name Joline Pearce.

Growing up rural Wisconsin, she spent a lot of time roaming the woods and fantasizing about new places. Adventures took her to Oregon, Michigan, and after a stint teaching in France, she moved to New York City, where she stayed for the next 15 years. There she acquired a pair of graduate degrees, a husband and a career as a librarian. An avid runner, reader, and cyclist, she lives in Maryland with two budding readers and her real-life romantic hero.

BOOKS BY CARRIE LOMAX

Historical Romance
Married Off by the Duke

The Spinster's Secret Scoundrel

The Wild Lord (London Scandals Book 1)
Becoming Lady Dalton (London Scandals Book 2)
The Lost Lord (London Scandals Book 3)
The Duke's Stolen Heart (London Scandals Book 4)

Twelve Nights of Scandal
Twelve Nights of Ruin
(Christmas Duet)

***Virtue & Vice* Victorian Historical Romance Series**
Belladonna
Annalise
Rosalyn
Justine

Forthcoming in the *Virtue & Vice* series (2024):
Cora
Isabelle
Rose
Jane

Contemporary series:
Say You'll Stay (Alyssa & Marc)
Say You Need Me (Janelle & Trent)
Say 'I Do' (Bonus Novella: Fiji Wedding)
Say You're Mine (Olivia & Ronan)

Fantasy Romance written as Joline Pearce:
Falling Princess
Eternal Knight
Queen Rising
Crimson Throne

Visit www.CarrieLomax.com for details

Printed in Great Britain
by Amazon